ROSES

&

PRICKLES

ROSES & PRICKLES

A NOVELLA

CHIZITERE MADELEINE NWAEMESI

ISBN: 978-978-970-794-2

Published in Nigeria in 2024 by LIBRETTO Publishers

LIBRETTO PUBLISHERS LIMITED
HEADOFFICE
Office R7, Owode, Lagos Garage,
Shopping Complex, Oyo, Oyo State, Nigeria.

BRANCHES
Edo | Abuja
Tel: +234 (0) 807 834 6790 | +234 (0) 813 044 6615
Email: librettong@gmail.com | publishing@librettong.com | info@librettong.com
Website: www.librettong.com | Bookstore Website: www.books.librettong.com
facebook.com/librettong | instagram.com/libretto_ng | twitter.com/librettopublish |
linkedin.com/company/libretto-publishers-ltd

Dedication

To every youth yet unmarried.

Author's Note

You can choose your partner, but kids cannot choose their parents. The quality of your child's well-being is entirely your responsibility.

Contents

Preface

Africa has the highest sickle cell disease predominance rate in countries such as Nigeria, Cameroon, the Republic of Congo, Gabon, and Ghana.

About 300,000 kids worldwide are born with sickle cell disease, according to WHO. Nigeria leads with the highest rate followed by other Sub-Saharan countries.

This disease can disrupt a patient's education, employment, psychological and social development. As a youth expected to make more informed choices, your choices should include considering a partner with genotype compatibility. This story is an insight into the marital anomaly prevalent in our present world.

One

THE SUN IS OUT BY 10 am: a good sign and pleasant weather. You sit idly in the backseat of your black Ford Edge, counting down on time, brooding over your next big move. Staring ahead into the rear-view mirror, a perfect face masked up in honey brown shades of artistry complementing each other on the different parts of your face stared back at you. Your neck is bare, but for the lacy neckline of your dress, hugging your collarbone tightly.

These are what you would have done suitably years ago: dress up and marry a man who is willing to swim through a lifetime of storms, regardless of what the waves bring. Having messed up your first chance of making things right, you consider today a second chance. Your eyes grow heavy with liquid. You look away from the mirror to fish a white scarf from your purse. Reminiscing your past is nostalgic. But what is a human without a history?

In most cases, the past has guided the future – a constant reminder of where you fell or where you might fall again if great care isn't taken in ordering your steps. The first time you experienced a day like this was nine years ago when love defeated doubts, when you thought love was all that mattered. Did it not?

~~~~~~

NNAMDI WAS YOUR CHILDHOOD ENEMY. The first day you saw him, he was a wailing boy of about eight or seven, and you were about five or six. His mother was a slender, tired-faced woman dragging along the boy whose wailing sent out unruly arrival chills.

Your mother was anxious to meet and know the new neighbours, so she slipped into her lemon Dunlop footwear and went downstairs to welcome them. You perched on the balcony, expecting to glimpse everything as the strange faces packed into their new home that year when an egg was sold for twenty nairas. You didn't know how your mother managed to tame the wailing boy, but he stayed with her while his mother directed the arrangement of their properties. You would later learn that he bore Nnamdi.

The next day being a Sunday, both mothers dragged their grudging kids to church, two streets away. Church; wide fenced, interlocking tiled compound, overly decorated altar, pastor and his wife in shiny clothes, seated at the far right end of the altar, overdressed women, underdressed men, white chairs arranged before service, clustered after service,
~~~~~~

your mother screaming the loudest amen at the slightest provocation, and ushers in orange flip jackets always standing. It all bored your nerves. Being mandated to sit and stand for so long, observing the same order of things every Sunday, bored you out. Your eyes darted around amidst the prophetic acclaims and praises, searching for the wailing boy and his mother whose beauty fascinated you. When your eyes finally met his (cold and calm), his lips parted to reveal his tongue, pulled down most annoyingly. You didn't forgive such a silly gesture, so you became enemies.

It was the kind of childhood you had, climbing up the balcony to stare at each other with sneers and smirks on your lips, hard against each other. Your older brother never understood why you both always hated each other, and you never understood too. You knew him as the boy always hanging on their hibiscus flower-decorated balcony, either munching on crunchy peanuts and cheeseballs or constructing paper kites that never fly, sucking Capri-Sun as if his life depended on it or wailing. On the days he cried, you took great advantage of his grief to wag your tongue in the ugliest manner. This always infuriates him, and he reacts by flinging any reachable towards your direction until his mother emerges to soothe him. You were most grateful for the excellent distance between both buildings. If not, you might have lost an eye, at most. Each two-story was distanced enough to park cars in between but close enough to see your neighbour frowning.

Ms Lucy, like your mother used to call her, is a woman of little words, peaceful or somewhat reserved, rides the best jeep in the compound, wears flowing silk gowns, and always sponsors Mothers' Day parties for all kids. Nnamdi was the last of her six sons; that was all you knew about her family. Sometimes you wondered who would inherit all her flowery silk gowns and shiny jewellery pieces. Why buy so much silk and gold when there's no you to leave them for? You used to think. Then you wished she had you in mind. Jewellery! Silk! What more can you ask for?

One summer you spent with your father in Kaduna, the wailing boy left Abuja and returned just after you concluded your first degree. At first, you didn't recognize the wailing boy who always lounged on their balcony until his old habits gave him away. It was a breezy evening, and your mother had gone out when you stood on the balcony attending to your phone, trying to be productive in a WhatsApp forum where you were invited to teach young entrepreneurs the basic business etiquette they should cultivate. It was your first time handling such a class, making you all nervous. There was so much to feed the hungry starters. You paced the balcony countless times to steady your anxiety before you looked up to find the most beautiful male you had ever seen lounging on

Mọ Lucy's verandah. After how many years? You were mildly anxious about the new man but returned to the task ahead. Then nostalgia hit. There was something about this demeanor, new but old and striking. You looked up again, and there he was, staring at you. Nnamdi! You gasped. He was still staring when you rushed back into the house, loathing your precious (most valuable at the moment) woolen cropped top and skimpy skirt. You should have worn something better. And why was he staring like that?

It took a few weeks of sidestepping each other before he accosted you.

'Flawa,'

His voice tasted like Naija jollof blessed with abundant aromatic spices and chunks of well-seasoned goat meat dipped in a hot sauce of British accent, served fresh out of the grill.

You smiled, battling with the thousands of butterflies that had sprung and began creating a nuisance in your taut belly. He will later tell you how encouraging your smile was and how much growth you have undergone. You were amazed by how he still called you 'Flawa', a moniker he initiated in past years to spite you.

'What have you been eating?' he asked

'Jollof rice and dodo'

'What have you been eating?' you asked, giggling like an early teenager.

'Everything consumable in England,'

You nodded slowly regarding him. 'So, that explains your disappearance.'

He smiled, revealing his perfect dentition again. The butterflies in your belly resumed prancing. So much had happened to Nnamdi physically. Save for the grin and eyes, it was hard to reconcile this grown man and the wailing boy on his mother's balcony years past.

'So, do you still cry?' you asked.

'Hmmm, no, but I can make you cry,' he winked. Your cheeks grew stiff.

'No. Stay away,' you rubbed your blushing cheeks.

Despite the warm familiarity, there were few expectations surrounding the events' outcome, yet his persistence instilled a glimmer of hope. No puffery but you have never been so glad you met a man.

After camping in Kaduna, you redeployed to Abuja even after Emilia assured you there were shrubs of law firms sprouting in Lagos who wouldn't think twice about discussing your salary if only you could bless them with your application. You knew Lagos was a crazy city from everything you read and heard about it, and you were not the type who gave in to cowardice quickly. But you didn't settle for the little faith you shared with Emilia immediately. You went back to Abuja to spend some time with your mother, handling some administrative work in her firm during the day, waiting on the verandah in the evening for Nnamdi where you spent most of your time smiling, dreaming about your bodies. Then one weekend as your mother was away in Kaduna on her monthly visit, you bathed and oiled your body assiduously, held up your hair in a bun, and disappeared into Nnamdi's room.

In your twenty-two years of little life experiences, hanging out with men who sent chills down your spine, kissing the overzealous ones, dating and dumping the available ones, nothing prepared you for what love truly is.

Whatever happened in Nnamdi's room— large like yours, sparsely furnished, bedspread that smelt of oranges, television on mute, ps4 game set cramped on a wide stool under the cable stand, an easel right under the air-conditioner, a blue rug with fur that caressed your feet—made you smile into the mirror when you returned to your room. His room was chilly, but you were warm. It wasn't just about his warm breath against the tender folds of your neck, the dampness of his bare palm on your butt cheeks, the ardor in the emotional transactions, the wet kisses he lined your body with, or the exhale of relief afterwards. It was in the way he paid attention to you like a quadratic solution that needed constant memorization, the way he listened to your endless unnecessary tales, trying to keep your mouth busy, but most importantly, his attention on your face. This was not familiar; somehow, you felt it in your fingertips.

There were days you hung out at Tweeters, a fine restaurant in town, to taste the intercontinental dishes that he recommended and indulge in wine tasting while discussing mass emigration, the loss of career professionals, and the effects on different sectors of our economy. It was worth the extra hours you spent on your face, creating little magic with brushes dipped in palettes, liner, and lip frames.

The second time you visited his room, you let him undress you, then sat on a high stool close to the window, naked but for yellow lingerie, with arms draped over your chest, cupping your breasts with palms. The streaking sunlight illuminated your silhouette. He set up the wooden easel at the opposite end of the room and sketched every contour of your features dextrously. You held that moment tightly to heart, and as you studied the finished drawing, you knew you would guard it jealously for as long as life allows.

Two

THE WORKLOAD AT YOUR MOTHER'S firm has risen well within the past months, and you were beginning to question your future in such an environment. The time came for Nnamdi to return to England. You were crestfallen and forfeited your February salary for your father's cosy duplex in Kaduna. Sentiments aside, you don't have to work for your mother so hard for peanuts at the end of each month. Staying in Kaduna was like being cut off from the rest of the world. There was no occasional opening of gates and honking of cars now and then. Your home in Kaduna always exuded so much peace, quiet, and comfort that there was nothing else to ask for. Except for your father's morning activities before work and the usual barking of dogs when he returned a little after nightfall, there was no other awareness.

You could never wrap your head around the fact that both parents live apart, speaking to one another once a week or so but never missing their summer vacation. After one of those summers, things began to fall apart between them.

You grew up watching your mother defend people in the courtrooms in a gown that cracked you up. Watching all the dramas that unfolded in a place where 'order' was the number one rule was strangely fascinating. Things you never imagined existed playing out amidst a surge of emotional outbursts, intelligent defence, professional pleas, threats, exposures, freedom, and sentences. Sometimes you searched the faces of those who swore oaths with palm placed on a Bible or Koran and wondered if there were repercussions for perjury.

After each court session, you trailed after your mother, dragging her handbag while she carried her briefcase, confident on the days she won a case, ashen-faced on the days she lost. This was her usual programme, shuttling between states and cities to represent strangers who paid for advocacy. Most weekends, she was home talking to her friends on Skype, standing on the verandah asking Ms Lucy about the wailing boy or sharing common interests in flower species or recipes for banga stew or soup, moi moi, carrot cake, coconut bread, cookies or Ghana Jollof. Other times, she punched furiously on her tablet or skimmed through countless journals and stacks of papers, each with at least two scribbles of whatever information she intended to put down in her slant-dancing handwriting.

It was too early, but you knew all these kept your father away: the mad state of books pulled from the libraries and abandoned on the bed, the uncanny neglect of household affairs, and long nights spent in the study with eyes buried in books. For him, it was madness. He couldn't put up with such madness at close range. So he completed his duplex after you turned seven and asked your mother to move in with him, which she opposed.

'Kaduna is too far, and you know it!' she vented. You found solace in both homes, each with a part to offer. They couldn't come together, so you had to get it. You and Vincent, your brother. This time around in, as there was no urge to return to the tan-walled home in Abuja, you remained in Kaduna, applying for funded and unfunded graduate studies programs abroad. It was long before the National University of Singapore offered you a place in Business Law (partially-funded). You left shortly during summer that year, gleaming at your future.

Three

DISARRAY. THAT WAS THE FIRST word that struck your mind when you came home. At the airport that day, while you waited for the baggage carousel to deliver baggage finally, you watched the preteen, a long-haired girl who clung to her mother. They were sharing delicious whispers that made them giggle so much. Her peach-coloured top hiked above her belly button to reveal her taut gut. It was lovely and strange. You didn't enjoy such PDA with your mother.

When Henry, your best cousin, appeared with a welcoming wide grin, you stiffened. He was more muscular than you could recall. The t-shirt, which hugged his torso, was quite revealing. After 14 hours of skimming through old books, stuffing your ears with R&Bs, drafting journals, and drifting from woolgathering to deep sleep, hugging anybody was the last thing on your mind, but you threw him a shoulder punch before thumping his back lightly. Henry's driving was smooth, just as your mother said, and that was why she sent him. She thought it was best to send someone familiar. And you sensed 'family' in her *familiar*.

It was easy to see through your mother. On the days she quarreled with her husband, it was evident in her vacant eyes, untidy hair, and bouts of tired sleep. Like fake harmattan, the tiny space created for family affairs vanishes. The air remained stale until things were cleared up.

Henry swerved across another Honda but blue, pedaling into a brake as you got to the traffic lights, with a few uniformed men clustered under the bright light. Like impending doom, the sky darkened and rumbled.

The street you left three years ago accommodated more than permitted. New restaurants were lining up like experiments. New buildings standing tall and firm. A plaza here and there. Power generators generating bangarang from each corridor, constituting a nuisance. New faces loitering. Familiar ones growing older. On impulse, you thought of returning to the airport, mind shut to Henry's pleas until you board a plane back to Singapore. But then you smiled at the impossibility. The temperature in your mother's Honda made your skin crawl.

'I will fix the AC tomorrow' Henry said.

You turned to stare at him thoughtfully, surprised he read your mind.

'You're our serious Oyinbo now. You shouldn't get used to the heat.' You smiled.

'Vincent is in Turkey now. Did you know?'

You shrugged.

'Flawa, you didn't reach out all these years,' he moved to squeeze your left thigh.

'Don't tell me you finally drowned your voice in fresh yoghurt.'

You forced a short laugh. 'I am tired, Hen.'

His efforts at striking up a conversation were understandable; something he was very good at but of all people, Vincent? C'mon!

When you drove into the premises you left a long time, it took concentrated eyes settling to absorb the changes in the buildings. It looked as if each story decided to take a step forward. Ms Lucy's car tarpaulin was almost a rag: her jeep, now old, and scratched headlamps. Nostalgia overwhelmed you.

Disarray. Yes. That was the state of home. Your mother sat on the single couch with a plate of sliced avocados under her chin, tufts of hair held up in a loose bun. Her eye bags were darker than the rest of her face. The blades of the ceiling fan moved lazily, interrupting the bulb's brightness under its wings. Disarray hung in the hair like Dove air freshener, the one your mother used to buy for the household. Henry rolled boxes towards your room. Your eyes followed him, concerned about the state.

'The house help cleaned it thoroughly today' she said coolly, stuffing her mouth with a slice of avocado. So now, everyone reads your mind? Is that what you have become? Pellucid?

'Mummy, 'you moved closer and soon felt each other's warmth.

'You need to rest, 'she said, almost in a whisper. 'Henry made pepper soup.'

You smiled. Henry's pepper soup was a special treat.

The room you left for a long time suddenly felt small and overly furnished. The large inbuilt closet suddenly seems too large. The reading table was fixed beside the door that led to the corridor, and the thick red Italian rug was gone, now replaced with cold tiles, a good thing. The bed housed new sheets and a blanket, thick enough to use as a shield against the AC on cold nights. Disarray. It nagged your mind. So when your mother brought in pepper soup and corn jello in a fancy tray with iron handles, you asked her what was wrong.

'Nothing happened, Rose.'

You admired your mother's eloquence in courtrooms, her ability to twist, transform, mend, and deliver statements and speeches in whichever desired form. It was magic. In her crisply ironed shirt and glasses hanging loose on her nose ridge, she accused and defended so perfectly with great poise. Then once she got into the car finally to go home, she removed her glasses and rubbed her eyes till they turned red, undone the first two buttons on her shirt, let her hair fall, and flung her briefcase to the backseat as if it all had been a heavy burden that would pull her down the next minute.

'Fasten the belts, Rose,' she would say before she drove off.

'Mummy, something happened. This place is like a funeral ground. Where's Vincent? How is Dad?'

'Vincent is in Turkey now. Your father is trying to fix him up with a job.'

'Vincent did not tell me, 'you shrugged.

'It was sudden. When he settles, he will talk to you.'

She reached the flat screen television and ran her forefinger on the rim. 'Does it mean this house help cannot clean anymore?'

Nnedi has been in the household since you were a teenager, but she was still the 'house help'. No matter how hard she scrubs bathrooms or tends to laundry, your mother wouldn't dwell on sentiments. Nnedi is her house help. But you called her Ms Nnedi as a sign of respect which you felt wasn't enough.

'Your father left, 'she said and angrily pressed the bell beside the light switch. A dishevelled Nnedi appeared.

'If you love your job, you have to ensure you do it well. Okay?' the scolded cat nodded, stunned. She hovered until she was waved away. You understood your mother's ploy to distract the sadness that might lodge between her chest and stifle her. You wanted to tell her that this wasn't a courtroom where she controlled the minds of others. This was you, her only daughter who knows what she knows, even better than she does. When you decided to take up your mother's career, it wasn't to be like her or better than her. But it was what you loved to do. Even in all the strain, it was easy for you.

'To where?' you asked, settling on a couch.

'He left us, Flawa. The divorce procedure has been messy, but we are pulling through. I will get every single penny I deserve from him.'

'What?'

'You should rest. We will talk tomorrow,' she responded, sauntering out before you could express any further shock.

The thought of losing your father made you understand a different kind of failure. Was it a failure? Who failed? Both parents. It was as if you waited an eternity for that day, the day everything would come crashing. You knew that kind of marriage would come crashing like plastic cups used to stand a tower. You traced Henry to Vincent's room a little after midnight. He cuddled up a pillow on the bed with his back to the entrance door. You stood antsy in pyjamas, unsure why you were there, if you should be there, but your heart craved old warmth, something different from the distractions you abandoned, something of greater compulsion and consequence. The last time you were there with him, Vincent had walked in on you.

'I can't sleep, 'you said when he roused from sleep to find you staring at him.

'Flawa, 'he stretched a yawn, surprised.

You snuggled up to him. He removed the pillow and pulled you into his arms. His stale but warm breath gently caresses your cheeks.

'She said my father left,' you muttered

'Hmmm'

'How long?' you asked, sitting up.

'As long as I have been here this year'

'How long have you been here?'

'Since Vincent left'

'Vincent…we haven't talked in two years. I don't know what to do with all this news.'

He reached out and drew you into his chest. 'Now that you're here, you should focus on your mother.'

His cologne filled your nose. You wanted to move, bury your face in his neck for as long as the night allowed, but you simply let him hold you. The night Vincent walked in on you both, you were on top of Henry, moving slowly, rhythmically like he taught you, damning the consequences. It was as if the world halted for two great sinners. The moment was evergreen. That was the first time you understood the nature of breaking things. Broken things will forever remain broken, no matter how much you mend them. His flash of anger constituted moving objects, of fury, of tension. And that was it. A breach in love, compassion, bond, and everything siblings could be. It became safer to love from a distance.

Henry nudged you. 'You should sleep' his sleep-induced voice filled your ears. An unfathomable urge to fuck him took over you. But there was something different about Henry. He doesn't entertain such desires anymore.

'You're seeing someone now,' you said, half questioning, half knowing, willing him to deny.

'Flawa. Let me put you to sleep,' he began to run his finger on your cornrows where hairs parted to reveal a pale scalp. In the early morning hours, you were still cuddled up to his chest, and he was lightly snoring. You did not lose him entirely.

Four

YOU MOVED TO LAGOS. IT was better than working for your mother. Much better than watching her drown more in liquor with each new day. You found little assuagement in Emilia's quiet apartment in Maryland. She was the only one who hasn't changed much to your detriment after years. You should have gone to Kaduna, but your father sold his house, closed his soap factory, and moved to Ghana. Before he left, he married his beautiful, lithe mistress and relocated with her. That was your mother's anger. Your father was cheating. No. Cheating feels heavy. You didn't like associating him with cheating because you were in Kaduna countless times and never met any other woman. He never mentioned any other woman. There wasn't any strange scent or body wash in his closet or bathroom—no extra towel. No undies. Nothing! If not for his busty cleaner who visits once a week, your father had no other company besides his children. So when the news of his marriage came, you were taken aback. Still, it was hard to say he was cheating because you thought your father was a gentleman who prioritizes his family. It was strange and unsettling to realise you didn't even know him enough. He was seeing another woman. Yes. It feels lighter that way. That was your mother's anger. He was seeing another woman, and he married her to replace her. And he was ready to move to Ghana to be with her because she had a growing textile business in Accra. That was your mother's anger. He was prepared to sacrifice for someone else but never made any for her.

'Am I stupid?' she asked you one day after strenuous hours at work. When she drove in, she didn't descend. The music in her car blasted while she sat there nodding to the beat. You had watched from the window for a while before meeting her. It took more than three raps on the glass to call her attention.

'I am beginning to feel stupid. Your father creates this gap between us and expects me to fill it up. So I'm supposed to shuttle between Kaduna and Abuja to keep a man who keeps another woman. I don't know why men bend the rules and think they can just walk away,' she shrugged, throwing up her hands.

'No consequence,' then she began to cry, her shoulders heaving. You stood unmoved. You always blamed her until that day. You thought it was her duty to move, go to her husband, and unite you all. You viewed your father as the lonely one and your mother as insouciant. You blamed her so severely until you watched her cry. It was revealing to discover she had so much bottled up.

'He has to pay every penny I spent on the both of you. Every single penny! Maybe I might fix myself up, or maybe not. I don't know,' she said finally, picking up her shoes from the floor mat. After that evening, you watched her recoil back to her shell. No more tears, no grieving, just silence.

The shrubs of law firms in Lagos were almost trees, and it wasn't easy to get interviews anymore. But you were called by Maurice's firm, the same place Emilia works, after five months of submitting hundreds of CVs and wallowing in self-deprecation. Slowly, you fit into the hurdles of the crazy big city, paid for an apartment in the same Maryland, and moved in.

You were sure Emilia had put in a word on your behalf, sure she had something going on with Benjamin, the chamber head. It was evident in how she smiled extra for him, brewed coffee or tea for two, ditched the loafers in her handbag, and wore heels throughout the day in a new gait and extra gloss to the lips every hour. You watched her with amusement.

Soon you were placed in an office where a large transparent glass demarcated your cubicle from Emilia's. You adjusted to looking forward to the days you appeared in courts and countless case trips.

Five

WHATEVER JIDENNA LACKED IN WORDS, he made up in looks. Long-legged, pale, hairy, and beautiful in the way his nose sat straight in the middle of his face in accordance. You met him in an elevator. Yes, an elevator. Not in the way you have seen in some Nollywood movies; the type you and Emilia go to cinemas to watch in your varsity days, sitting next to each other with a big paper bag of popcorn and medium-sized bottled drinks demarcating your arms, your eyes glued to the projected screen, grinning and giggling, and comparing the romance playing to the ones experienced. It was different.

You were almost late for lunch when you got in the elevator, offering prayers and hoping moi moi didn't finish by the time you got to your favourite kitchen. Then a man in a plain black blazer and a pair of black Converse sneakers joined on the second floor. You paid him a compliment not because you know anything about quality blazers for men or because you were particularly interested in light-skinned males but because you read something about casually paying people compliments. He smiled. Smiled again. You smiled, too, because when he smiles, all you could see was Henry. His smile was contagious, and that was it.

'Roselyn' you said curtly, extending a hand for a shake because you weren't in the business of waiting until asked.

'Small Chief,' he pursed his lips, taking your palm. A storm of amusement bellowed in your belly.

'Why small?'

'We all start small, don't we?' he winked, and immediately you decided that you wouldn't mind kissing him right there in that uplift. To hell with social ethics, conduct, whatever.

On the first date, you shared a cup of Cold Stone at Lewis. The second time, you played snooker at Bachelors Sports Club. The third time, long minutes were spent skimming through Quenette's restaurant's menu but settled for wine tasting at last. It was all good; the delicious novelty, the fluttering butterflies in the belly, the emotional assurance, presumed validity, and consistency on his part. It felt like love and you gave in, wholesomely.

Jidenna proposed in early April; that season when rain hasn't fully returned, when bacteria form tiny black dots on the tender skin of yellow mangoes, when the sun shines hot and the air blows cold. That morning, you had stirred from sleep to find him kneeling beside the bed, his hands outstretched, a slim band housing a diamond stone, held firmly with a thumb and forefinger. It was beautiful. You knew it was beautiful albeit your hypnopompic state. It was something memorable, so memorable you built a large space for it in your heart and laid it there carefully, accessible enough for constant revisiting. It was what you wanted; a nice job, good marriage, and every other thing that follows. But what followed? Grief.

In your pubescent years—you and Vincent—your father developed stronger punishment measures every time you erred. The first time you shared your mobile number with a boy who bugged your phone incessantly with calls and sick-love messages, you were about 15. This is what he did; he stripped you to your underwear and lashed you until your butt cheeks turned a bright red. It was so humiliating you swore he hated you. "When you see sin and walk right into it, you burn your feet" he said afterward. When Vincent swapped a school day for a football match in Otako, he was subjected to harsher lashing and starvation. Later on, burnt boots. That was the end of football for Vincent. "When you see sin and walk right into it, you burn your feet." Your father told him afterward. You both got fair shares of burnt feet on numerous occasions.

Eight months after engagement, you chose a gloomy Saturday in early December and walked down the aisle. Vincent did not come. He could not leave his job. Your father acknowledged your invitation but did not come. That day, your mother sat on the pew behind, rearranging the ribbons placed on your hair the way she wanted it to be, flanked by Emilia. The exchange of vows was solemn, unsure if the promises made to each other would stand the test of time. There was lodging in your chest but you could tell why.

Three months before marriage, you had gone for the necessary medical tests and it was bad news. Jidenna was AS genotype, and so were you!

'Couples with same AS genotype are not encouraged to get married' said the dark doctor whose eyeglasses were as thick as glass louvers.

You didn't give up. Nothing was satisfying as getting a partner who is a fighter as you are. A partner who is willing to try no matter what the world gives. You went back to the doctor to weigh your chances.

'You're about to embark on a perilous journey. Having healthy kids is not guaranteed. It's all about taking the risk but the chances of bearing an SS carrier is twenty-five percent. Few survive it and their lives will be filled with pain and sickness. Let us take some time and think about all of these. Consider yourselves, you know, not just the kids' he cupped his palms to his mouth and sneezed gently.

'Both of you will be involved; the hospital bills, stress, and emotional trauma of losing achild to this sickness. It will surely be devastating. I believe we can agree on this. Else you're not planning to have kids at all' he smiled, tightly.

'Our kids are very important' you told Jidenna later.

'Of course! Rosey, but we can do this. Forget that doctor with his half-sight' he replied and you laughed.

'How can someone who can barely see tell me whom to marry?' you laughed harder.

'It is not always like that. There's nothing to worry about' he pulled you closer into his arms.

Your protest was feeble because love was the ultimate. Then, you went back to Abuja to talk to your mother.

'Eziokwu?' she got up from her seat and sat closer to yours. She took your palm in hers and caressed it for more than a minute before she spoke.

'You're my only daughter, and your brother is not talking about marriage in the nearest future. I am seventy percent involved in this. I don't want a second heartbreak, Roselyn. I need grandchildren; healthy ones, not the ones you would whimper and feel tensed up when they experience a slight headache. There are a lot of compatible genotypes out there. Men who might even be better than whom you have now. Sickle cell anemia is a dangerous one. Don't you know? Are you going to walk into doom with eyes wide open? You as a mother will be affected mostly. You have to rethink this marriage,

Roselyn. It will make you unhappy. Onyesikaọfụ, ọfụ!'

'But mummy, it doesn't always end like that. I believe things can work out well if we have faith and believe in positivity. We can avoid all of this.'

'Roselyn, what are you saying? Avoid what? Listen to me. I know you to be a stubborn type, but this is not the best way to exert it. This is a matter of life and death! For goodness' sake, be reasonable.'

She heaved a sigh.

'I understand you love this man, but you know love fades, so does beauty. But your children will always be there. Try and give them a better life. I will never deceive you. Rose, you're too educated to be reasoning like this. I will say no more, go and have a rethink and give me feedback. It is still your life to live, so you can as well live it the way you want.'

The officiating priest looked on with compassion. Did he know what you were doing? Did he know you were marrying a man your mother advised against? Is that pity in his eyes? Are you going to regret it? The lodging in your chest popped and formed a fresh boil. And with each word spoken, the vows felt heavier.

Six

A YEAR AFTER MARRIAGE, KACHI was born. A boy, full of life, beauty and innocence. It was a moment you couldn't trade for anything in life. The final result of many nights of heaviness coloring your mind, gorging your soul with love. A different kind of love. The kind of love you were willing to live for, to hope for, and to die for. Another two and half years passed before Ijeoma came. A girl; full of hair, light-skin and ample cheeks.

It was a rainy Thursday when you received a distress call from Ijeoma's class teacher and you were exempted from a court session that was supposed to commence by 10 am.

'Madam, we need you here immediately. Your daughter is having a health crisis!' her breath, labored and windy.

You dropped the phone in confusion, rushed out, and drove as fast as your ability could carry on. It was when you wanted to call your husband that you discovered your phone was left at the office, on your office desk. So the teacher had to lend you her phone to reach him. Thirty minutes later he joined you at the hospital.

'Where is she? Can I see her?' he asked in one breath. You gaped without concentration as he paced up and down the hospital lobby. Later he sat beside you and you determined not to shed a tear. It was not the first time incidents like that happened. You were already adjusting to the constant hospital visitations but each time, Jidenna hoped for the best while you prepared for the worst.

Ijeoma died the next morning. Those early hours of the morning when akara vendors have finished mashing and grinding beans. It was about the same time when your mother sends Vincent to go and wait on her customer so that once she scoops out the first set from the sizzling oil balanced on a bright cooking furnace, she wraps it up immediately for him before the morning rush began. An errand Vincent hated so passionately. But the family had to eat Akara. He had no choice.

The previous night, the need for an urgent blood transfusion arose. Unfortunately, there was no available donor in the entire building. By the time Jidenna returned from a journey of almost an hour to buy blood, the nurses were already covering her up. The two pints of blood fell on the hard floor and became a mess.

You sat by her and watched her dry cracked lips. Then you heard Jidenna sniffing and a lady moping the mess that splattered everywhere. Minutes dragged on as you stared at your three-year-old. A child is stolen by death. You reached out to remove the tiny curl of hair that fell across her left eye. The past weekend, you had set her head between your thighs and twisted the strands into curls but not without cajoles and promises of dozens of edibles. At least she died with new hairstyle.

Jidenna came to you after she was deposited in the morgue. You sat in silence for long, unsure of what next to do.

'We can't keep her there'

'Yes' he muttered.

'We will take her home'

'Rosey, we will come for her tomorrow, definitely' he reached out to rub your shoulders.

'I don't know why you are in such haste to put her in there. She might not even be dead yet. What happens when she wakes up?' you asked. 'You promised her a trip to Wonderland. Do you think Ijeoma forgets such? All those clothes I got last week, who will wear them?'

When you looked up, he turned his face away to hide the tears that dropped down his cheeks.

'Why are you crying? Is this how you give up on my baby?'

You looked away to see a nurse helping a pregnant woman get on her feet. You hoped she doesn't go in there to pass through all the necessary pain and in the end, let death snatch her victory from her. Then you thought you heard Jidenna say 'I am sorry' you smiled. Sorry for what?

Seven

IJEOMA WAS BURIED THE NEXT day, shortly after your mother's arrival, at the church cemetery. The officiating priest said a series of prayers before she was lowered into the freshly dug hungry ground. Slaps and thuds of the clammy red soil on the hard coffin wood and that was the end. A child you nurtured for three years was gone.

You discovered and joined Sickle Cell Moms Club in Ikoyi, after Ijeoma's burial. Every Sunday evening, you didn't mind covering twenty-three kilometers to attend meetings, health talks, and testimonies; whatever it takes to save Kachi. Sometimes they held marathon prayer sessions and advised few hours with a therapist. Such advice infuriated you. They were trying to save their kids and yet here they are, thinking about themselves, (you shouldn't say but) the perpetrators of the problems.

It was on such evenings that you met Adaolisa, your schoolmate in secondary school. Adaolisa Ukpabia whose uncle sends all her stuff from abroad, ranging from house wears, robes, powder palates, undies, water bottles, and the fancy chocolates she used to share with whoever she chose. Same Adaolisa who always deposited a reasonable quantity of saliva into her water gallon after filling it with drinking water and shaking it thoroughly. Then she turns to you the onlookers and pulls out her tongue in a very ugly manner. Adaolisa whose menstrual cramps began on the assembly ground and she rolled the whole compound in her immaculate white shirt. An act that made Ms. Chetachi—the school-born again teacher—to start praying fervently and speaking in tongues until the teachers who understood what was happening intimated her, and she couldn't contain her loud hiss.

'Ordinary period! Is that why she is rolling on the ground? I thought she was possessed' she hissed again.

Ms. Chetachi. Maybe it was incidents like that and numerous of her lack-of-compassion actions (the same compassion she preached) that made you not mourn her death as you should the death of a woman who taught you for more than four years.

Adaolisa in Sickle Cell Moms Club! Pheeewww! Small world! You avoided her in the following weeks until she accosted you one evening after health talks.

'Aahnn Roselyn Nwaka! This girl, you haven't changed.'

You hadn't expected such openness so you smiled tightly, fidgety.

'Adaolisa, you have serious hips now ooh'

She laughed heartily. Her silky hair parted in the middle of her forehead fell to her open cleavage. You walked onto the little garage where your cars were parked side by side, unknowingly.

'I am surprised you have been in Lagos' she said after unlocking her car.

'It's been long years, Ada' you smiled again.

'We should talk more, Rose. Maybe next week after prayers.' You nodded in affirmation.

Your membership lingered and straightened, soaked in deep faith for the little redemption you felt in other people's testimonies, observations, and motivations. Once a month, you took Kachi with you, afraid he might be stressed if he went every Sunday. Sometimes, his father volunteered, but rarely. On the Sundays prayer sessions were held, you ended up with heels aching so badly that you wondered for a misguided minute if these people think prayers alone could change the genotype of these kids. It was pointless. Feeding on such hope was pointless but you fed on it because what else? Nobody had a better option that wouldn't cost a fortune or risk the little hope you basked in.

One morning, you eavesdropped on Jidenna speaking to your mother on the phone while he was dressing up.

'Ma, it would be best if you made it fast. I think things are getting worse' he wedged the phone between his ear and left shoulder while buttoning up his shirt slowly.You stood by the door, rooted.

A short pause.

'Very bad ma' he continued. 'I can but your presence will aid a lot.' Another pause before the call was ended.

Before mid-afternoon, she was at your door chiming the bell. Gratitude filled your heart because, after Ijeoma's burial, you hadn't seen her. Her Burberry wrap blazer clung to her willowy body most sensually.

'I wasn't expecting you' you wrapped your arms around her waist and registered a light peck on her left cheek.

'I stopped by to check on you. I am supposed to be in Ibadan but that can wait till tomorrow.'

You smiled, mildly amused by her smooth lie.

'What have you been doing with yourself?' she asked, peering into your face then she stroked your hair.

'I have been good, just stress from the workload. I am supposed to be in Ibadan too but I canceled. I can't leave Kachi.'

She nodded thoughtfully. 'Where's my grandson?'

'This is siesta time mum'

'Must he observe siesta?'

'I wouldn't say I am surprised at you because I know you're just trying to pull my legs.'

'In our time, there was nothing like siesta.'

'It doesn't make us all victims' you grinned.

'Rose, 'victim' is not an appropriate word.'

After a long silence, she adjusted to her seat and opened her bag.

'Your box is in my room'

'As usual' she smiled. A cheeky smile that made her rosy cheeks more pronounced. Then brought out her diet crackers and bottled water and kept it on a stool nearest to her. She continued fumbling inside her bag until she produced a bag of fruits and a handful of chocolates.

'Thanks, mum. How did you know I need fruits?'

"I am your guardian angel, besides, it's for my grandson, not you' she removed her glasses to wipe the frame.

'Your husband called me' she wore back her glasses.

'He did?' you asked, unwrapping a chocolate bar.

'He said you joined a Sickle Cell Moms Club.'

'Yes.'

'Does it help?'

'You think it doesn't?'

'You have a beautiful family; your loving husband, your dear son. That's all you need. You are still grieving if you have to cover such distance every Sunday to find peace. Nothing will bring back the dead, Rose.'

'Whatever it is that club has to offer, I need it, mummy. If Jidenna thinks it's madness sitting around digging the obvious, he is entitled to his opinions. Was that why he called?' you arched your brows.

'It is for…'

'Mum, please. How is your best friend?' you switched, spitefully.

She shrugged. 'She is in Paris for vacation.'

'You didn't join her this time?'

'Where did I see such money? Have I finished my bungalow in Apo?' she adjusted to a sleeping position and shut her eyes. 'Her daughter is sponsoring everything.'

Tinuke. That was her name; thick, tall, and bossy. She was neat to a fault; everything that belonged to her had to be dazzling. Growing up, you often wondered why your mother kept a Yoruba friend but then you realized that there is much to accord to personality than tribe. Her only child, a medical doctor in America was a spitting image of her. Every year she would go for vacation abroad, mostly to America to visit her daughter who hardly came home. Her daughter who was in her early 30s was still unmarried and the mother never talks about it. She never talked about grandkids, unlike your mother. When your marriage came up, she went furious.

'It is better you remain unmarried' she said leaning on her seat.

'And be like your daughter?'

The riposte was not enough. You wanted something icier to douse the tremble her sermon stirred in your nerves.

'There's nothing like happiness, my dear' she didn't give you the satisfaction you craved.

'If being single makes her happy, who am I to obstruct that? Don't see it that way because the time will come when she will be better than you if you go on with this marriage. Marriage is not always the bus stop because aside from the euphoria of a new marriage, bigger responsibilities awaits the couple when the novelty wears off. So why do you consider marrying a man of the same AS genotype?' she asked supporting her chin with her bent wrists, her slender fingers harmonized with her long acrylic nails.

'Well, that makes me happy too' you replied nonchalantly.

She smiled and turned to your mother who sat away peering curiously into her record book.

'Roselyn is so much grown now'

Your mother flashed her a half smile and went back to her puzzle. By 'grown' you know she meant arrogant, brash, uncouth. When you were left alone with your mother, you complained about her unnecessary divulgence in her friend and demanded some privacy for you and your husband-to-be. After Ijeoma's death, she reached out with heart-melting condolences and guilt engulfed you.

Eight

ONE OF THE FIRST THINGS we should have been taught about life is fragility. Holding onto things too tightly breaks them, not holding tight enough is worse. It is like garnering sunflowers on a windy evening in a garden. Holding on too tightly squashes them and when you leave them out in the basket, the wind scatters and carries some away. Lost things either return dented or never return at all. We don't have an in-depth knowledge of this life we are living.

You waited for a few days before you questioned Jidenna about the distress call he placed to your mother. It was mid-evening. He lay propped up against a pillow, scrolling on his phone.

'Why did you call my mother?' you asked quietly. Though you should have just told him outrightly how unnecessary it was and will be if he kept calling your mother to come and look into your face but didn't know how to start.

'Have you looked at yourself lately?' he asked.

'Why?'

'It is a good thing we talk about this again because you need to stop going to that club. You're losing yourself gradually, Rosey.'

'There is nothing to lose here, Small Chief. It is still pardonable that you're not making any effort. But it will not remain pardonable if you keep divulging my mother. She has her problem and it makes me feel helpless. I don't like it.'

He turned to stare as you sat up on the bed. His large eyes pierced your forced rigidity.

'Rosey, see the hollow starvation has dug on your neck. You fast from Monday to Sunday, push your career aside, and travel every Sunday for as far as two hours just to read out scripted prayers and discuss death. What are you not telling me?'

'I will say nothing about this again. But you must understand that I am making efforts. Kachi cannot just die like that. I have gotten a lot of tips from this club and it brings me mind development. You either accept it or you accept it. Every day you sit at your desk in your establishment! Your establishment! And bury your eyes in laptop screens. I am the one who grabs excuses every damn time to fix situations. Do you even want us to lose this child?'

'Rosey, please' he got up, adjusted his shirt that rode up to his mid-back and headed out of the room. 'I will fix dinner.'

In the weeks that followed, you tightened your dedication to the SCMC like toddlers tighten their fingers around anything they could touch. On the first Sundays of the month, the matron shares out a prayer template that covers the month. And there were numerous prayer points printed on it. There was also the ritual of accepting new members that tripled with each new gathering. Their faces were expectant at first, bubbling with hope that declined as the weeks sped by. Second Sundays were for health and diet talks and more prayers and a few other activities that took up time. The third Sundays were mainly for motivations and testimonies and announcements of a cessation of the pain of some victims that has grown so acute. On such days, when a woman or man or anyone stands with a bowed head, the tension in your belly clamps down on the bladder which brewed hot urine. After such announcements, you hang your heads low and say a short prayer while ruminating. It could have been you but it wasn't. You say tosoul to steady the psychogenic tremor that had begun rioting in your hands. The last Sundays were for counseling sections and open interactions which was heavily backed up with long prayers and a summarization of the monthly prayer intentions template.

Adaolisa lost her five years old girl. It was the third Sunday of that month. That day, after church service, there was a mild weakness in your bones that spread and multiplied but you did not give in. After a lunch of coconut rice and grilled fish, you put Kachi behind the driver's seat and headed to Ikoyi. The cloud, moody and rumbling promised a downpour but was hesitant to fulfil it. When it was time for testimonies, no one had anything to say or maybe they did but declined disclosure. You would later know why. When the time for testimonies passed, Adaolisa stood and walked unsteadily to the rostrum. A silky black scarf wrapped around her cornrows down to her long neck. She was still adorable albeit with her heavy eyes and faded black gown. For a misguided second, you wondered why she came herself, why she had to stand up there and act like she owe you all a first-hand narration.

Her slender finger wrapped around the microphone as she clutched it. She stared at the small congregation of heads with keen, misty, and tired eyes fixed upon her, words failed her.

'My princess...' words failed her again. You felt she shouldn't have been up there in the first place.

'My princess is gone' she began to sob. Most of the women cried too. You locked the emotions in the locker of your chest and counted down on time. Later, they circled her, the women in different shades of beauty and condolences to offer. When you hugged her, her chest heaved rhythmically and her lips quivered.

'I shouldn't have married him' she said and you were stunned. 'You can't blame me. It was like a last chance. I didn't think I could ever find such peace.'

'Don't blame yourself, Ada. This is one of the things we can't control.'

'No. It is my fault, Rose. My princess is gone and it is my fault.'

You hugged her again, tighter this time as she broke down. You had seen the girl a couple of times; thin-faced like her mother, frail and sickly pretty. You derived much pleasure in watching her cling to her mother every time they were together that you imagined Kachi that way but your son was not the clingy type. He was already developing a mind of his own at six and you often wondered if he would grow to hate you, his parents.

After Adaolisa left, you put Kachi beside the driver's seat and got in. And for long minutes you drummed your fingers wildly on the steering wheel while waiting for the air conditioner to cool off the hot air in the car. Your phone beeped. Emilia had sent the travel tickets to Kaduna for an ex-senator's case. You were to be present in court by Tuesday. It was a political case and as much as you hated to meddle with politicians, the offer was usually mouth-watering and heavy. You leaned over and hugged your son passionately. The loneliness you saw in Adaolisa's eyes crept up into the depth of your stomach. Fear nagged your spirit throughout the drive home. There are ones we cannot afford to lose.

Kachi was already dozing when you got home. You carried him carefully into his room and prepared his bath. The cloud darkened outside. The whistling of the wind roughly caressed the windows and wrestled with the doors. You bathed Kachi hurriedly and fed him a little quantity of the leftover coconut rice before putting him to sleep. The rain began to fall, like pebbles hitting a hard surface. You stood before the mirror in the bathroom and peeled off your clothes slowly. Jidenna was right. The hollow in the pit of your neck has deepened more. Your breasts drooped as you unclipped your brassiere. The wind banged against the window panes harder while you pulled down your undies. There was something about the weather that brought momentarily pleasure to you. It reminded you of the night spent in Kaduna with Henry. The lukewarm water spread goosebumps on your skin.

Nine

A WOMAN CAN BE A slave to a man's thrust. You know this because you're such a woman. Sometimes when you watched Jidenna hold classes with his foreign tutees, flexing his arm muscles, analyzing, dictating, questioning, or any of the rest he does each time he was sharing knowledge on his laptop, you always cannot help but wonder how you got here. The traits he shared with Henry could never be missed, not even a bit. But were all these hospital trips, death, and anxiety worth it? What was it all about? Love? Sex?

You stood before the mirror and observed your unclad body. The skin on your tummy was thin but the linea nigra wasn't entirely faded and that made you think of pregnancy. Maybe, the next one will be free from this madness, this blood-sucking sickness. Then you smiled because if you would be pregnant again, you'd be needing a guarantee from God himself. Balls of precipitation hit hard against the bathroom window panes, a reminder of the raging downpour. You turned on the water heater and refilled the bucket in readiness to bathe.

While you waited for the water to heat up, you rehearsed the speeches prepared for the next day's court case by heart. Collaboration and brainstorming wouldn't be left entirely to you. Assigning more than two barristers to a case strengthens courtroom presence and for the first time, you were grateful for such situation.

Emilia was making sure you didn't abandon your career completely but she will never be able to fully understand the circumstance. The thought of going to Kaduna stirred up the little meal in the tummy and bile rose to your throat. You dreaded it after your father left the urban center. At first, when he sold his house, you did not believe it. You borrowed your mother's Highlander and blackmailed Henry into driving you to Kaduna. The shiny black gate securing his house was gone. It had been replaced by a gigantic red one. A shrill-voiced dog barked when you knocked. You sighed. It couldn't possibly be Kritsha. Kritsha was gone. Dogs are not your favorite pet but Kritsha was always an exception. You did not stop knocking until a stone-faced man opened up. Then you asked about your father. The man's stale breath compelled you to hold your breath and his words bore disappointment. The house has been sold. It no longer belonged to Chief Fidelis. There were new occupants now. You patiently waited until he turned his back to your persistent "Are you sure? Do you know how I can reach him? What ofhis new address?" before wrapping arms around Henry's neck and weeping.

That evening, as Henry combed Kachia town for a suite to settle for the night, you sat beside him weeping while the sky darkened and rumbled. You cried until he finally settled for a suite his friend had recommended. It felt like your heart was placed on a slaughter table and diced into a hundred pieces. Your father fought so much with silence that he even did not think of divulging you. While in the bath you cried until Henry slipped in. The rain fell thunderously on the zinc sheets and against the window panes. The weather wore a mournful look of greater grief. You did not stop his experienced fingers when they traced the small of your back or stop his wet tongue from circling your taut nipples. His hot breath incited you. It was something you had bundled and burnt years ago but that night, when grief overcame, you found the burnt spot and dug up the ashes. You rekindled the ashes. It filled the air like incense and swirled your heads. The cause of tears changed when he began thrusting in his familiar rhythm that pacified and gorged you with pleasure. You cried again but not for your father anymore. You cried for all your wrongdoings, for the feelings you cannot talk about, and for being a slave to a man's thrusts. The day Henry wedded, you lay on Emilia's bed, brooding. If you hadn't lied about an emergency trip to Nasarawa, you should have been in attendance with your mother.

You turned off the water heater and turned on the tap. You scrubbed your skin furiously, hoping to scrub out the dirt of death that had settled on your pores at the club. One time ago, you read something about death somewhere. In the excerpt, they illustrated how contagious death could be; how quietly a carrier could pass it on to other unsuspecting victims without prior knowledge. Then, you had hissed at how superstitiously the writer reasoned but that day in the bath, you scrubbed until you were well convinced and satisfied that any agent on your skin must have not survived such cruelty and died. Your body was covered in soap lather when Jidenna slipped into the shower. His fingers gripped your hips gently.

'We should send you to a fattening room.'

You loved the way his warm breath caressed the skin on your neck. You smiled and reached for water to rinse your face then spent the next ten minutes sponging and rinsing your bodies. Before he slipped in, you held the shower stand and arched your waist as his fingers buried themselves deep in the flesh of your hips. When he began moving, you thought of Henry and tears filled your eyes. With each deep stroke that erupted a thousand specks of weakening pleasure, you hated yourself. You hated yourself for desiring that kind of comfort; for not mourning princess.

Ten

JIDENNA LEFT LAGOS FOR IBADAN on the eve of Kachi's sixth birthday. Before you began fretting out, he had filled you with a hundred and one reasons why he shouldn't miss this special programming course he would tutor in Ibadan for three months and because the money could handle Kachi's health expenses for the rest of the year, you consented.

On Kachi's birthday, you baked sponge cakes and fresh pineapple juice. You also let him tie his shoelaces and he made a clean job out of it. It was a quiet birthday not only because Kachi wished so but also because his father was somewhere in Ibadan, standing on a podium and addressing strangers. The first time you accompanied him to Abuja for a friend's official book launch, you were surprised at how foreign everything they discussed was to your ears. It created a hazy edge between the both of you. While you sat and ruminated and observed, loneliness crept in, that was when you decided not to accompany him to any such event or even the occasional classes he held once a while in the universities where he was invited to share knowledge. The atmosphere wasn't as accommodating as you had envisioned and the worlds of knowledge were very unalike.

Emilia came around later that day, carrying gift bags and chocolate cake for Kachi. Her aura permeated extra goodness; her dimples sat extra deeper as she smiled, her hair glistened with a new sheen, and her dress; a wrap yellow piece that hugged her full skin in an adoring manner. She waved a shiny diamond ring consciously across your face, and giggled endlessly.

'Who?' you asked

'Who else?!' she laughed.

'This should be the first office romance that led to marriage I have experienced.' She laughed more.

'I will take him to my parents next weekend'

You admired the way the band gripped her fleshy ring finger.

'What is his genotype and blood group?' you asked and kept a straight face.

She raised an eyebrow and spread out her palms, unsure of what to say. At last, she found her tongue and kissed her teeth.

'Everybody cannot be you, Rose' she set out the cake on the dining table. 'I love with my brain.'

'Well, I am here if you need any marital advice.'

She roared in laughter, this time hitting the table gently with her palm. You wondered what was funny but then remembered she was still battling with serious euphoria of her engagement and forgave her.

'Where is our birthday boy?'

'I made sponge cakes, Nnajide. He has eaten more than enough today. He will have the cake later.'

She ignored you and ascended the stairs to fetch a probably sleeping Kachi.

Eleven

KACHI DIED. YOU THOUGHT LIFE could be pampered and nourished with so much love that the owner forgets about losing it. You thought yours was different from Adaolisa and all those women who stood at that podium to talk about death. You thought God could show you a little mercy.

It was a cold Friday night in April after a frenetic march in Jidenna's fifth week in Ibadan and he agreed to return for the weekend. '…Just for the weekend' he emphasized this many times. Earlier that day, you scrubbed your face with a sugar face scrub, waxed your pubic hairs, and let your body soak for long in the bathtub after baking and cooking. Then, wait like those years, when you waited on your mother until you heard her familiar shrill honk. It was refreshing to wait on him and you recognized that same feeling the day you waited at the Murtala Muhammad International Airport. Ijeoma was a toddler and Kachi was almost three. You held onto Ijeoma's tiny palm sticking out of the baby's carrier, gripped Kachi's hand, and stood on your toes, hoping to catch a glimpse of his head. Time passed. You waited till the arrivals dispersed gradually with or without any welcome until Kachi snatched his hands and ran off, screaming 'Deeddy' towards a direction you were forced to follow. You were looking ahead but he was looking underneath. Then you smiled when he came up with Kachi on his shoulders and realized how beautiful such moments were. It was gratifying to have someone who can wait for you.

But you waited in vain. Jidenna had missed his flight in error and it was already late to make new arrangements. Palpitations nagged you but were shrugged off.

'First thing tomorrow morning, I am on my way to Lagos' he assured you.

'I baked a cake for you and...' your voice trailed off.

'Really? Egg yolk?' the excitement in his voice wasn't unnoticed.

'Yes.'

'You are not happy.'

You held the phone to your ear with your left shoulder while fixing the torchlight battery.

'Rosey' his voice was small.

'I'm here. I was trying to fix something.'

'Okay, but you don't sound happy.'

'I was hoping to see you today' you sighed

'I'm sorry, Rosey. Forgive my carelessness' he sighed too.

'We will be expecting you in the morning.'

'Alright Lolo Small Chief. I will be home before you wake up'

You smiled knowing he had bowed while saying that.It was twenty minutes to midnight when Kachi started losing breath. You noticed his fever earlier which was tended to before bedtime hoping it would subside but then pains began to spread out again and he gave in to crises. You called Jidenna and he suggested calling the nearest help. Emilia was probably in Port Harcourt so there was no nearest help. Confusion played on your reasoning. You ran out forgetting your car keys only to remember them halfway down the stairs and ran back. By quarter past midnight, you were honking madly at the hospital gate.

Jidenna arrived very early in the morning; that time when the fog was yet to clear from the atmosphere, that time when the nurses ran routine checks and administered drugs to admitted patients. You were too weak to welcome him so when he came to the waiting room, you wrapped your right arm around his left thigh and squeezed before he left to see his son. Then you asked yourself thousands of questions but received answers for none. What if you lose the only eye that is indebted to blindness? How will you see?

'Have you seen him?' you asked when Jidenna returned.

'He kept murmuring he needs air.'

'He has been saying that. I turned off the air-conditioner and opened the windows myself. I don't know what else to do.'

'We need to go home, at least to get some cash. I didn't come with enough. You need to bathe and eat too. It's almost 8 am.'

'I'm not hungry. You can go and get the money. I will stay and look after him'

'The nurses are here to do so. Let us go, okay?'

'No' you relaxed into the chair and shut your eyes.

'Rosey'

His persistence drained and kept you mute. He stared for a few seconds before he left. You opened one eye to stare at his retreating figure and felt exasperation surge up in your throat. You swallowed bile. Severally, you tried to pray but the words crumpled and got stuck in your throat so you called your pastor and then called Emilia later. She was in Jos and would be back in Lagos by noon the next day. 'Everything will be fine' she assured you.

It was mid-morning when Kachi demanded food. You had roused from a short nap that didn't last for more than fifteen minutes. It was a tired sleep. The kind you give in to after Mondays' court sessions. You didn't hesitate to stand before bending over him.

'What will you eat?'

'Cornflakes'

'Cornflakes?' you repeated.

'Get him rice' Jidenna said.

'Allow him. If he wants cornflakes, I will get him that, but I will also get you rice, okay? You will eat that later' you smiled in a bid to convince to him and luckily, he nodded and looked on, pale and sickly.

On getting home, you boiled rice hurriedly and took out an unopened cornflakes pack from the upper section of the kitchen cabinet where packet foods and eggs were stored. You went into the children's room to get a lunch box to pack the cornflakes. Then got tins of liquid milk, apples, and chocolates from the refrigerator and packed everything into the lunchbox before dishing the boiled rice and tomato stew in a small food flask.

When you were done, went back to the room and caught a glance in the mirror before grabbing some bottles of water and threw them into a plastic bag you had collected from the kitchen and hurried downstairs, hoping you forgot nothing important.

On getting back to the hospital, you parked side-by-side with Jidenna's Lexus, took out the bags, and headed straight to the children's ward. Bile formed a soft swell in your chest and rose to the throat. You shook it off, affirming it came at the wrong time. Your son needed to be fed.

Jidenna was speaking to a petite nurse in low tones when you entered the vestibule that led to the children's ward. He seemed startled on sighting you but fortunately for him, you were too absorbed in thoughts to see through his uneasiness immediately.

So, to cover up, he turned to you and reached out to collect the food boxes while the nurse looked away and excused herself.

'You are here already! I wasn't expecting you back so soon'

'Is he sleeping?'

'Yes. No, he was about to when I came out to see the doctor'

'What were you discussing with that nurse?'

He ran his left palm over his beard and back to his head. 'She was telling me he needs multivitamins.'

'Okay' you replied, attempting to move away, but he stood, unmoving. 'Are you okay?'

'I am fine, Rosey. I am just tired. I am really tired' his voice strained as he ran his palm over his head again.

'Your eyes are misty' you noticed.

'Really? Yeah, is it?'

Again, you attempted to move into the ward, but he stood there. You looked into his face.

'Leave my way or are you going in with me?'

'Rosey, we need to talk' he said, and scratched his head roughly this time, confused.

'Kachi requested cornflakes, remember. He might lose his appetite. Whatever we need to talk about has to wait.'

'It can't wait, Rosey. It is urgent.'

'What do you mean?' you flared. He held onto your wrist and squeezed gently before dragging you aside.

'What is wrong, Jidenna?' you asked again where you stood a few steps away from the entrance that led into the lobby. He adjusted the straying braid attempting to fall out from the loose bun in the middle of your head, still holding your wrist. His eyes were suddenly red.

Your mind raced. This silence was familiar, yes! When Ifeoma, your mother's little sister (though not so little at 24) was hospitalized after a rough home abortion, Ndudi, her 'fiancé of three years' came to see your mother three days later and stood at the door even after he was asked to sit. His eyes were this red. That day, you sat at the dining section of the sitting room, stealing curious glances at him. You had always thought Ifeoma was making a mistake by getting involved with him until that day when he stood there and waited for your mother to come out. Somehow you saw through his unspoken grief but didn't want to share his guilt. When your mother came out, they whispered in low tones until she screamed 'Say something! Just say it! Kedụ ebe Ifeoma nọ?!'

He held onto her hand tightly. His eyes grew heavier and heavier until he broke down and fell onto his knees.

Your mother turned to you. 'My sister cannot be dead' she shrugged, walked back to her room, and banged the door shut. Ndudi knelt there until you came and patted his shoulders albeit the old awkwardness in between. For a long time, your mother would often lament 'She should have kept the baby. Is it not a good thing? All these standards that society set for us always damage people.'

Jidenna's eyes grew heavier and your knees weakened. He held you still, saying nothing. You stare at each other, dazed.

'You're crazy' you muttered quietly.

'I know. I'm also stupid, I am so stupid. I feel stupid'

'Where's he?'

'It doesn't matter now. He died twenty minutes ago.'

'Where's he?!' you seized his collar.

'Rosey, wait…come with me' he turned and walked back into the long corridor of about six rooms. You rested your head on the wall trying to steady your vision. Your wobbling knees gave way and came down heavily on the hard floor. You couldn't stand the sight of another corpse of your child so you stood and walked out, steadily, into the vestibule and out of the hospital building, towards the gate and out of that damned atmosphere where people gave up their lives for the sins of others.

Twelve

KACHI WAS BURIED IN THE church cemetery. Your mother flew in from Abuja early that day. His classmates and schoolmates were flanked by teachers who you thought were too bright for the burial of their pupil. Emilia wept throughout the time when the Rev. said the necessary prayers and performed holy rites on the casket. You did not cry, instead watched everyone; watched their hands wipe tears in quick succession and listened to sighs and murmurs. Jidenna walked about like a ghost, unsure of what to do next. He avoided your hard stare. You avoided any sort of eye contact with each other and harbored unspoken grief. People crowded the graveside. Different kinds of voices contributed to the sonorous:

"When peace like a river, attendeth my way, when sorrows like sea billows roll. Whatever my lot, thou hast taught me to know…it is well, it is well with my soul."

The cloud gathered and was about to unroll rain but the voices rose higher and up until tiny drops began drizzling.

Thirteen

SILENCE. SILENCE IS POWERFUL AND destructive depending on how it is weaponized. But it's more destructive to fashion silence as a weapon against grief. It feeds on the soul with claws until there's nothing more to feel.

You waited until Jidenna went back to Ibadan before resuming your Sunday trips to SCMC. While the atmosphere bustled with prayers and activities, you sat and let your eyes roam around for Adaolisa. You would later learn she severed her membership and left the country. You resolved to find her on Facebook which you never did. You might be a constant reminder of the pain she left behind. It will be fruitless, you knew because everything about SCMC was fruitless; the prayers, fasting, trips, faith, lots of faith and hope, hope! It was crazy. Every time in attendance, you felt wrecked and empty. Whenever the affected ones climb up the podium to speak, you grip the chair hard and bite into your lips.

Jidenna finished his course and came home with a plan. He was going back to Ibadan to establish because he thought he found the right audience for all his tech problems and solutions. He met a South African who was willing to team up with him. They would make a good team. They were both tech wizards and if time permits, they could move to South Africa within the next three years and develop a new branch there. His skin pores evaporated with great zeal as he gesticulated with his fingers. You watched his eager face as he talked and talked and you wondered where he buried his grief.

That night when his wet kisses grazed the hairs on your arm, you put your life on the tip of your tongue, it tasted bland then you let your mind wander off. You let his fingers seek, pull and poke until your legs were ready to receive him. His thrusts were feverish and short and shallow. You wrapped the lemon-silky robe around your lean body and sat up.

'I'm not moving to Ibadan' you re-tied your headscarf and got up, got to the door, and looked back. He lay sideways, snoring lightly.

The next afternoon, as you parked your handbag for the regular Sunday trip, he paced the width of the room, fuming.

'We need to talk, Rosey'

"You want to stop me from going to the club? Is this not a joke?'

'I know all of these are heavy for you. That is why I gave you enough time to dwell a bit. Firstly, I will call your mother so she can help pack out Kachi stuff from that room. Then you will come to Ibadan with me. Let me take you away from all of these for a while.'

'Firstly, my mother is in Jerusalem. Did you forget? Secondly, I don't want anyone near my son's stuff. Thirdly, I am not going to Ibadan.'

You stood before the mirror and adjusted your turban. Bitterness lurked in your eyes. Then you grabbed the car keys and snatched up the ready handbag. Before you came home in the late evening, he was gone. But he came again the next weekend. He kept coming until he realized it was impossible to convince you otherwise. So one weekend, while you sat arranging Kachi's photos according to age, he packed most of his personal belongings and left for Ibadan.

Fourteen

EVERY MORNING, YOU SCHEMED THE food timetable—drafted on a hard lemon-colored paper and pasted above the microwave—with curious eyes but never settled for any. Instead, you fill Kachi's water flask with liquid milk and throw it into your bag. At the office, you get submerged in work and forget entirely about your poor milk. The weeks rolled by quickly and folded into rough months and it wasn't long before a year passed. Emilia still wore her ring with confidence and you became inquisitive.

'My mother doesn't like him' she shrugged. 'She thinks he is too conservative.'

'Conservative?' I don't understand.'

'You know…' she gesticulated

'I don't know! Ha! Emilia Nnajide. Does your mother remember that we are not getting younger?' you reclined on the twirling seat with squinted eyes.

'Give this to the librarian' she passed a sheet of paper with almost unintelligible handwriting. 'Let her find the case files and give you. Forget about my mother and what she thinks, Flawa.'

You acted on impulse. You took a sick leave from work and booked a late evening flight to Ibadan.

Later, you would understand that some situations and confrontations were better buried like Jidenna buried his grief. The last time he came home was three months ago. His software programs were kicking off. He was getting more recognition with the influence of his 'friend' and he smiled with great hope. You soon realized his 'friend' was quite anonymous and there was always this glint in his eyes whenever he talked about him.

Jidenna was not happy you landed in Ibadan without prior information. But he arranged a taxi that brought you to his doorstep. It was a long block of about three occupants who had a spacious sitting room and master bedroom each. You watched his mass of hair.

'You keep hair now.'

'I just want to change my looks a bit. No big deal.'

His muscles filled out under his sweatshirt and you felt driven by desire, a strong desire to let him fill you up until you are gorged of satisfaction.

'I heard you handle Senator Ibekeh's case?' his words interrupted your ardent desire. You nodded.

'He made me tell a lot of lies'

He laughed shortly and said 'It is your job.'

You smiled in affirmation. After he insisted you pack out Kachi's stuff, you let him do it but not without hoarding most of his shirts and toys. You couldn't afford to lose him entirely.

That night he made shredded beef sauce and white rice but food had long lost its taste in your tongue. You nibbled on the food while he wolfed down his. His cutleries clattered on the ceramics plate endlessly and you thought of Kachi. Sometimes you expected Kachi to return a punctured plate to the sink but it was just a clatter, a habit. The humming of the refrigerator accompanied the plate clatter. The room walls were bare except for his portrait that hung above the twelve inches television. The blue bulb illuminated the room so well that everything was blue. In the shower, you waited for him to hold you the way he usually did back home but he stood at the far end of the bathroom and lathered his body furiously. You looked away and stopped expecting.

The next morning, you slept till past seven. Then roused and shut your eyes still. You tried to organize your thoughts that were beginning to run in zigzags. You didn't make a mistake by refusing to settle in Ibadan. Kachi died because he was destined to die. Princess and all those kids you lost were also destined for the same. You could still make amends. You would leave that crazy city and move in with your husband. A year has passed. You could adopt two kids and raise them. You would apply for jobs in the contiguous areas. But first, you would talk to Henry. Your mother told you he moved to London with his wife. There was no easier way to contact him other than Facebook.

You lay in bed until Jidenna left for a seminar he was organizing in UI. The tea he served had evaporated all its vapors so you took it to the kitchen sink drain and rinsed the cup afterward. The refrigerator resumed its humming immediately after electricity was restored. The tiles were chilly under your feet as you searched for a laptop. You found his old **hp** after a lazy search and dragged the charger together with it.

You regained access to your Facebook account but Henry's old account was no longer in existence so you were forced to ask your mother. *Did you know his mother returned? My sister is unbelievable. Isn't Henry your best cousin? You should call him instead.* She sent his number minutes later but you left it in the inbox and procrastinated. It felt better spreading it at the back of your mind like you would the kerchief on those torn leather seats in the long bus ride to school before you sat. Then you searched for any old files that you might have left on the laptop but found none. You were about to search for his playlist when a Signal message notification popped up. One Claudia. She was expressing her regret over the sudden emergency trip back to South Africa. It seemed like she was shying away from confrontations but she didn't want to mount so much pressure. She believes in him. She was missing him. She was hopeful the break will help him resolve and decide if he wants them to be together.

You drew back from the reading table and opened the rest of their entire chats. Their box was almost empty but for previously shared documents and a few old messages. You clicked on one. A tan-haired olive skinned lady; with bulging eyes, thin lips, and long fingers that wrapped her left arm as she smiled at the camera. She visited Zanzibar and thought she did send him pictures. *Zanzibar is nice.* She was hoping to visit the Peace Memorial Museum. You opened the second document. A short clip of her in white lingerie; her ample breasts clung to the white piece that barely covered its cleavages, her labia majora demarcated in the middle. She would be going to Ghana next and they could go together. A lump formed in your chest and swelled and spread until you could no longer swallow bile. The laptop screen light went to sleep first before the lights went out and darkness descended on everything. The humming of the refrigerator stopped. You thought about light and decided that we can only choose one; light or darkness. Light and darkness can never be compatible because of the power each possessed.

You waited until he came home by past three in the afternoon, then microwaved the leftover rice and served him. He was excited about an eight thousand dollar gig from Tanzania, courtesy of his 'friend' but will be paid in instalments because it would last for months. He could take you to the Bahamas. He laughed. You pointed out that the Bahamas could cost more. He knew but he wanted you to know he loved you. You smiled.

You didn't wait for him to finish eating before you asked about Claudia. He stopped eating and stared at the opened laptop on the small reading table for long minutes. He continued eating. Claudia was the friend he has been telling you about. A South African, a tourist, and a tech expert. A fellow tutor in the three-month course. A divorcee.

'Did you sleep with her?' you asked and slouched. He did not answer. He was sorry and that was what mattered. He would make amends if you let him. His cutleries clatter continued until it grew really offensive in the heavy silence that had descended in the space that you wondered how he managed to find appetite. His son died hungry and he was suddenly ravenous? How did he treat important matters so lightly? How could he get over Kachi's death so quickly? You picked up the laptop and smashed it hard against the tiles. He was calm but he stopped eating. That was all you wanted; for him to stop chewing like a mammal and end the goddamned clatter. You picked up the cracked case and kept hitting it against the hard floor until the floor cracked too, until the lump in your chest flattened and grief wore you down. The loneliness that drove you to Ibadan spread its wide arms again and embraced you. It was the only one who could stand with you in light or darkness.

Fifteen

YOU ASKED FOR A DIVORCE. He was calm when you told him. Even if a gun was pointed to Jidenna's head, you realized, he would be calm. He was always calm even in the face of the scariest storm. It was supposed to be a smooth divorce but his non-reaction bored you so much. You felt reckless, reckless enough to know what you wanted; a messy divorce.

'Why leave him?' your mother asked

You cannot stay. It's been eight years but you cannot stay. Emilia implored you to reconsider but what does Emilia know about marriage? She has been in a state of confusion about this marriage thing for the past year because she was fucking one retired bank manager in Port Harcourt and they had agreed it was purely non-committal. He was the one who funds her dollar account every month but she loves Benjamin. What she felt for Benjamin was tender and undecided; and the old man; brittle and closeted. You cannot take advice from one who is in a fix.

That afternoon after you destroyed his laptop. He left you there crumpled on the floor and went out. You began searching his closet and boxes for Kachi's pictures. You only found the one he took at

Landmark Beach. His back was turned to the camera. His hair was full and curly. During that period he had taken a serious liking to the child actor's hair on Nickelodeon. On the day he was supposed to go with his father to a barber's saloon, he hid away in his room. He wanted full hair like the boy on the television. His father was upset but you let him grow his hair until it was full enough to smear with a relaxer. Afterward you changed his moniker to **Little Princess.** The skin on his neck was lighter than his arms. His legs were rooted in the white sand as he spread out his arms. His shirt was flying. You had taken the picture with the mini camera bought during a trade fair in Singapore. It was his most beautiful picture so you printed it into several copies and enlarged one.

That was the only picture that belonged to Kachi, the rest were his and one from the numerous you took in school abroad. You shouldn't have allowed him to move to Ibadan. It was your fault that you married a beautiful man whom ladies want to pull away from his family and keep to themselves. Then you understood his silence over the months. You did not relent in the ardent desire to crack smooth surfaces, to break everything you could so when he came home later that night, you told him you wanted a divorce and for the first time since Kachi's burial, you saw real distress in his eyes.

'A marriage without kids, Rose, is not worth having but I love you. That is all I can say.'

All he can say? He said literally nothing. You thought.

You accused him of neglecting his son and breaking his vows. He accused you of neglecting him. He wanted you to move in with him. You could get a better job easily with your powerful CV. You guys could have another kid. This time you would seek professional advice. Something can be done. There are chances of having healthy kids. He had plans but you refused to move. You were grieving for the dead and neglected the living.

'You don't know what it takes to bring a child into this world' you said quietly.

The day Kachi was born, he was in Lokoja attending to an emergency appointment. You wanted him to be there but he claimed it was an emergency he couldn't help. 'What about me?' you asked. So what does he even know? Does he know how much of a mess you were that day? Does he know about the discomfort? Does he know about the splitting pain that accompanies a baby's arrival? Does he know about the tears? Sweat? Blood?

Back home in Lagos that Friday, you trashed all the packs of expired cornflakes in the kitchen and put down Kachi's wall portraits but the loss still hung heavy in the air; in the large sitting room, in the kitchen, in the room, in the restrooms, everywhere.

When the lady cleaner came on Saturday, you dismissed her. You would clean yourself. But you did not clean. You never cleaned. Jidenna came to pack the rest of his things on Sunday and offered to do the laundry and dishes. You got upset.

'You should be in Ghana with Claudia. Did you forget?' you lay propped up on a pillow and dragged down the flesh of a banana with your teeth.

'Are you sure you want this divorce?' he asked. You turned to stare at him, cold and hard. He raised his hands in defeat. You lay in bed and ate bananas upon bananas while he packed until he left. Then you rolled up the bedsheets with the banana peelings and dumped them in the laundry basket, threw a black woolen jacket over your red handless jumpsuit, and drove to Ikoyi.

Sixteen

THAT DAY, WHEN THE TIME came for announcing the dead, you raised your hand. Everyone turned to stare at you, surprised. While climbing the podium, you tripped over one of the three steps and almost fell. People gasped. One of the male voluntary workers helped until you mounted the podium.

'My son Onyekachi died' you started. 'Crises came before midnight and I rushed him to the hospital because it was the kind I could not manage. I left him with his father because he wanted cornflakes but before I returned he has been covered up.' A pause.

'My baby died hungry'

Sighs rose in the air, murmurs followed, and then silent prayers. You were not finished yet so you gripped the microphone hard for support until the noise died down.

'What is the purpose of this club anyways?' people fell back in silence.

'The day before yesterday, it was Kola, yesterday Princess, today Onyekachi, whose turn is it tomorrow? Thousands of prayers but to what end? Women! To what end? Every Sunday, I drive from

Maryland to this place for redemption but there's in fact no redemption. Maybe we should be realistic. Why get into this kind of marriage in the first place? Why watch these kids slip off our hands? Kola, princess, Onyekachi, and many others I cannot mention.If not for the sins of you and I, none of them deserve to die.'

The murmurs rose again. The worker who has helped you ascend the podium came up behind you. You knew what he wanted to do so you ignored him.

'I did not go to the market to purchase babies!' you screamed into the microphone. 'They formed and developed here' you hit your abdomen. 'The kicks, the bonding, the stretch marks, I bore it all. Because these kids are supposed to be with us, to grow and look after us! They are the future we want; our doctors, nurses, solicitors, architects, artists, intellectuals, name them! Women! All of you here. Did we go through all of these to give these kids out to the wretched hands of death?

The worker tapped your shoulder lightly. You turned to him. 'Excuse me, I'm asking these women' you unclamped the microphone and descended the stairs. The worker stood transfixed.

'You think you have faith? Do you think you have the money? None of these can save them. If we could experience just a little bit of the pain these kids sustain, then we might be able to stop and ask ourselves if this is really love or madness.'

You dropped the microphone on the Terrazzo floor, walked in an unsteady gait back to your seat, slammed shut your bible, threw it into your Tote bag, crossed it over your shoulder, and headed out.

Amidst the rising voices, some women sat bound in their chairs, unable to digest what had just happened. They stared in astonishment while some argued. *Who is the bitch? She isn't the only one who had lost kids? The club should reconsider her membership. What does she mean by money cannot save them? My distant cousin paid for her daughter's bone marrow transplant and the girl is a doctor now. Is that woman mad? I think she has lost her mind.* They will never forgive you.

Voices rose, and arguments tripled until it was impossible to control them. Soon they began to disperse reluctantly but they would return the next Sunday which was majorly for prayers to cast and bind any spirit of negativity and death breeding among them. A loud amen would convey the hot spiced prayer up on the roof of the building where the scorching sun would roast it until it withered away.

The drive home was slow and delayed but your mind was drifting so you didn't even notice. By the time you drove into the garage, the sun has crept back into its hideout and dark clouds were beginning to gather and overshadow the bright one. You waited in your car and listened to *Orinoco Flow* by *Enya*. The music poured out through the speaker and filled the tight cold air. It felt like painful rashes on every skin pore, stinging you without mercy. You waited and bore the sting. What is an ordinary sting to death? What if you died? You could bear anything if Kachi could be brought back to life; even death. These thoughts raged and nagged until you turned off the music, but *Enya's* voice followed you until deep into the night. The jollof rice you made three days ago had been untouched for two days and you knew there would be no need to check the pot. The food was already spoilt.

The next day, you went to court and watched absentmindedly. You had gone to fulfil the office policy but while in court, you realized that you can as well break the policy if you wish. You have been here every Monday for the past seven years.

You were here when Ijeoma died. They had expressed condolences but of what depth? You were still here when Kachi died. What did they do to assuage the pain? They sent bouquets of fresh rose flowers and tons of condolence cards. That was the only Monday you missed work. Debbie delivered it to your doorstep. Debbie; the solicitor in office four, the one that never lost a case, the same one who removed a used tampon in the restroom one moody morning and forgot it on the sink. You met her in the mirror before you went into the restroom. It was such a gory sight and you notified her. Her mouth fell agape and her face crowded in thick furs of embarrassment. For the rest of that week, she avoided your pitiful eyes but you understood, perfectly.

Who even made these policies? Why were you so bound by it? You got up and left the courtroom. Outside you sat on the balcony pavement and waited patiently for the Bolt ride you ordered.

Seventeen

TWO WEEKS AFTER YOUR ABSENCE from work, you sat before your laptop and typed a resignation letter. You had spent the two weeks in your naked bed; scrolling through your social media pages, nibbling on edibles, swallowing sleeping pills, subjecting yourself to abnormal water therapy, drifting in and out of restlessness, reading without concentration, and listening to Enya's *Amarantine.* Then in the third week, when you were sure your mother would be at work, you dialed her office line severally until she answered.

'Mummy, I'm a mess' your voice had grown thinner and cracked.

'Roselyn,' as a newly appointed judge, you knew her schedule was tighter. The beauty in her voice seemed rejuvenated and it was music to your ears.

You sighed. 'I'm a mess. I left my job.'

She waited for you to say more but you didn't so she ended the call and booked the next available flight to Lagos. By mid-afternoon the next day, you answered to the chiming of your doorbell and there she stood in a red flowery gown that wrapped her willowy body and thick dark goggles covering her eyes. She embraced you; a hearty embrace that broke your spirit.

Back inside the house, she flinched at the stench in the kitchen and instructed you to call your cleaner. When the cleaner arrived, sleep had gotten a better part of you so your mother assisted in sweeping out the rooms only. By the time you awoke, dinner was ready and every nook and cranny of your home was sparkling. The balls of semolina you dipped in the white soup your mother prepared grazed your throat lightly as you swallowed each tentatively.

'I have booked our flight. You're going back to Abuja with me on Friday' your mother said in the middle of the meal and you nodded. When you woke up, you had found her peering into your face. 'You were struggling and crying in your sleep' she explained.

That night after she served you tea, she climbed the mini ladder in your library and chose *Felicity*by Mary Oliver. She read aloud slowly as you sipped the hot liquid quietly. While she read, she traced the lines with her forefinger like Kachi did on those days he read out questions from his workbook. She flipped the pages at intervals, ruminated on which to read next, and settled for the shorter ones. Her voice floated with the words and rhymes till its consistency lulled you into another bout of sleep.

The next day, she dragged you to Ikoyi marriage registry. Madam Tinuke's daughter was tying the knot with one Oladimeji. Both are doctors in America. Her mother had insisted they come home and wed after living together for almost two years.

'You know all these Nigerian Oyinbos. Always forgetting their roots' your mother filled you in. When you saw her, you marveled at her body size; tall and huge. Her caramel skin shone under the bright sunlight; her face beat; perfectly, and her fascinator; sparkling white. After the pictures were taken, the invited few followed them back to the hotel where they would be hosted. You prayed for everything to end quickly so you could go back to your bed, and sleep.

Later that evening, while you were in the restroom purging as a result of the vegetable sauce you ate earlier, your mother pulled down clothes from your wardrobe hanger to help pack. You returned to the room later and settled into an armchair.

'I shouldn't have married him' your voice was little but she heard you.

'Where's your pink traveling bag?'

'It is torn. I have a new one now. It is beneath those folded sheets. Brown colored.'

'You will need about a dozen clothes; three skirts at least and more trousers. Then shirts, polos, night wears, and undies. Just sit there and give me directives.'

'What do I do?' you asked, this time, louder.

'Nothing'

You watched as she folded the clothes into vertical lumps and placed each side by side in the open bag.

'This is what happens when you see sin and walk right into it; you burn your feet. You knew it was a thin line yet you walked on it. Nneoma, I told you this was going to be hard.' She only made use of your native name when she scolded you.

'As an adult, you don't do things anyhow you want; because when you make wrong decisions, the aftermath can be heavy. I blame no one else but you. Who am I to decide for you?'

You sat still and fixed your eyes on her.

'Albeit all these, you shouldn't have left him.'

'He left me, mummy.'

'Rose, marriage is never smooth. There will be disappointments and failures but it is not a good time to leave.'

A lump formed in your chest and you found it hard to breathe.

'It is just that you never find it easy to forgive.'

Silence ensued afterward as she folded and placed the clothes, vertically, to ensure the bag contained everything you needed.

Eighteen

THE WALL PAINTS OF THE house where you spent a greater part of your childhood have lost every glint of their recency. Ms. Lucy's shiny jeep was then old and washed. There were a lot of nameless new faces around.

Your mother's new help; a dark bony boy, had helped you settle in your room. Ms. Lucy had been sick for the past two years. Your mother told you how she moved to England to be with her son and for better treatment. But she was back and frail. One of her sons was home with her with his daughter. She didn't know how long they were staying because she thinks Ms Lucy will go back and this time around, for good. Your heart missed a beat for a second and began beating wildly. You could feel the insides of your stomach churn and move. Which of her sons is with her? You did not ask your mother.

You loved the peace you discovered in your chilly bedroom. Your old books were still on their shelves, your old shoes which your mother hoarded were still in their rank, neat and arranged, your gowns, also there in the wardrobe, old but still scented of your old perfumes. Some nights you stood before the open wardrobe and took these clothes to your nose and sniffed each for long minutes. Fond reminiscent.

One night you opened the closed boxes, went through their contents, and found a picture; you in a yellow swimsuit that barely covered your bum cheeks. Your braids fell across your mid-back as you posed for the picture. It had been taken on the day Henry took you to a private poolside party in Gwagwalada. He had taken several of that pictures but only printed one for you and backed the rest to his Google cloud. Before he took you to that party, he was just one of your maternal cousins who spent the greater part of his late adolescence in your home.

His mother (your aunt) had only nursed him for three months, then left him with her sister-in-law and disappeared abroad. Nobody knew the country she went to. Nobody knew his father. So your mother and her siblings took turns in raising him but when he became aware of himself, he decided to remain with your family. You took a special liking to him because he was a delicate young man. He made the best pancakes you ever ate and mixed the exact water temperature you loved for a bath. He helped out with mathematics and taught you new English words. It was harmless and innocent at first but one day while he flexed and massaged your toes, you felt a warm rush of liquid between your legs. It was the first time something like that happened but it did not bother you.

You waited until the day your mother took Vincent with her to grocery shopping. His eyes were fixed on Sandra Brown's *Charade* when you went into the room he shared with Vincent. You let him flex your toes again. Then you told him how you felt. He looked away but that did not make you relent. You wanted to feel more. A chance finally came one April in the year that you were admitted into University. Vincent was away in Uyo attending her federal university while you were home waiting for your Jamb results. You let him suck your toes gingerly until a wave of spasm swept through you. When his slender fingers glided in between your legs, you could not control the demons your body possessed but you told him not to stop. He went on to bury his face between your legs and you screamed as your legs shuddered in frisson.

The little affair lingered and progressed as you became insatiable. Whatever his tongue and fingers did to your body was evil but you assured yourself it was a necessary evil. One night in late June, he did not stop when you came. He knelt on the soft mattress and pushed your hips closer to his groin. You did not stop him as he poked with his penis until your vagina walls gave way, accommodating him. The sharp feeling of numbness suspended your thoughts, anxiety, and ecstasy. He moved feverishly for a few seconds, burst, and collapsed on you. His sweat tasted like fresh tears. You locked your legs around him and dissolved in tears. You did not get over the affair. It lingered for so long, even after Vincent walked in on you.

Your sleeping routine returned to normal in your second week in Abuja but you spent more time in bed and avoided the verandah. The doorbell signaled breakfast, lunch, and dinner respectively until you told the boy to call for dinner only. You could fix the rest yourself.

As the days passed, you offered to buy the groceries and clean out the deep freezer. He was reluctant but let you when you persisted. One sunny afternoon after a lunch of cold fruit salad, you opened your verandah to a little noise in Ms. Lucy's apartment. There were frantic movements, a man opened the door to their verandah, grabbed a carton of bottled water, then some foot wears and snatched a scarf off the hanger. In a flash of light, he was downstairs throwing these items into a car; a black Lexus. You watch him in wonder, trying to read through his panic. Your questions were soon answered as he carried Ms. Lucy down the flight of stairs and lowered her into the back seat of the car. A lady joined them, carrying a child of about four years on her chest. It took you several seconds of wonderment before you realized the man was Nnamdi. Goose bumps spread out on your pale skin like margarine on a slice of bread.

Nineteen

MS LUCY DIED. SHE HAD battled with Angiosarcoma for the past two years and finally gave up. Your mother sat on her favorite couch and wept over the weekend when she returned from a five days trip to Enugu. You didn't know she had considered the deceased more than an old neighbor.

You sat beside your mum during her funeral service in Agulu, her hometown, in your all-black attire. Your eyes wandered and scrutinized all her children but Nnamdi as they circled her white casket. You have been avoiding his eyes ever since you walked into the church hall and he looked up to see you. Prayers and hymns were offered before the casket was lowered into the grave. When it was time for you to leave, your mother walked up to him to offer her condolences once again. You felt his eyes bore through your soul but it was hard to avoid him anymore.

'Nnamdi, Ndo. Take heart.'

His eyes were sad as he smiled his thank you and bowed as your mother patted his shoulder. At the airport that evening, while you waited for the three hours your flight was delayed, he never left your mind . He was then a full-grown Nnamdi in all his goodness. The clingy little boy was grown, bearing responsibilities, burying his mother. What happened between the both of you held no water because he went back to England and the little romance died. None of you tried to rekindle it.

He came back to Abuja with his daughter after two weeks. He was moving to Jos by the end of the year because he was planning to officially launch his first art studio in Nigeria. He told you. You grew curious about him and he invited you over. He made greasy pancakes—nothing like Henry's— and served you on china plates.

'Your mother said you married and moved to Lagos' he asked after serving you.

'I moved to Lagos before I married'

"Oh. I married too but we're divorced.'

He went on to tell you about Aoife, his Irish wife who did drugs. He doesn't want to leave his daughter with an addict so he told the court about it when the divorce got messier and he was favored to be granted the custody of his child as the mother is unfit mentally and psychologically.

'I can imagine,' you sighed, though you had no mental strength to imagine anything.

'How about yours?' he asked.

'Mine?'

'Yes. Your marriage'

'I left him' you said quietly and picked up a slab of pancake. He nodded and asked no further questions. But you told him why. You told him how you lost your kids to sickle cell disease and how much it affected your marriage. He excused himself and returned with a clean canvas.

'Let's shoot' he winked at you.

He once told you about how he carefully penciled his mother for her 30th birthday. She had marveled at the magic her son performed on a canvas and couldn't contain the excitement.

'Nnam, you don't draw, you shoot!'

The word stuck. Shoot. It was shoot for his mother and you but not sure for his clients.

It had been his mother's best portrait. During her funeral, it was the portrait that hung over her casket.

He let loose your kinky locs, and let them fall across your shoulders. Your tank top suddenly felt too gummy for your slender body but you recognized the feeling and shook it off. A loc fell in between your cleavages but he drew it like that. When he finished and passed it to you, you stared in awe. It was a portrait so you asked him if you could take it. He declined because he was yet to paint it.

After your second month in Abuja, your mother offered you the head of chamber position in her firm. 'You cannot keep staying idle' she retorted when you asked her to give you some time to decide if you will remain in Abuja.

Then one early morning Emilia called crying on the other end of the phone.

'Benjamin called off the engagement' she sniffed. You sat up and pressed the phone tighter to your ear with your shoulder as you retied your robe and got down from the bed.

'Why?' you finally asked.

'He said he doesn't like the way I wore my lipstick, which is too bright, too unnatural, that my nails are mostly fixed. He doesn't like my homemade fruit juice, and my work clothes seem too tight and skimpy. He said a lot of things!' she voiced in one breath.

Your first impulse had been to laugh because you had never heard such silly break-up reasons in your life but you held it in. Careful. Careful. You warned your straying mind.

'He said a lot of unnecessary things!' she sniffed again.

'Do you even love him?' you asked, feeling reckless.

'I won't be crying if I don't want him'

'I am asking about 'love' not 'want' because I don't know what you are doing with that Port Harcourt old man if you love Benjamin. You should be intentional about what you want, Nnajide.'

There was a long silence that followed and realized you had been more than reckless in such a situation where honesty could hurt more than the actual problem.

'You make me look so stupid. I did not expect that from you!' she finally blurted and hung up.

You headed to the kitchen to prepare coffee refusing to think about what happened. That same evening, you made up after apologizing a thousand times.

Twenty

I HAVE SEEN THE WAY Nnamdi looks at you but I strongly think you should go and see your husband in Ibadan. Just go and see him, if things don't work out positively, come back and stay here in Abuja with me. I will pay you double of what they pay you at Maurice's' your mother said one morning while you were exercising. You clasped your fingers behind your head while lifting your torso slowly and said nothing. Then waited another two weeks before you booked a flight to Ibadan without Jidenna's prior notice.

You arrived in Ibadan by morning and booked a cab to his residence. Someone had begun growing hibiscus flowers in large red vases outside his small verandah and a wild random thought suggested Claudia. When you pressed the doorbell the fifth time, it wasn't Jidenna who appeared first. It was Claudia, in a blue piece of slinky gown that revealed a slight bump. The beauty you saw on that laptop that day was not a facade. Turmoil brewed in the pit of your stomach. When Jidenna saw you, he was apprehensive. He sent his mistress back in and shut the door behind her. Then he expressed his surprise.

He never knew you would come back but it was late because he was leaving the country soon.

'You couldn't fight for us'

Your voice was little and wounded. He caressed his head and sighed.

'You should never have left me' his eyes grew misty as he spoke. 'I am sorry about our kids. I just did not know how to mend broken things. And you were so distant, Rosey. I tried to break those walls of uncertainty but all my efforts were put off.'

'Is her genotype compatible?' you asked

He began to wipe his eyes. 'I love you, Rosey but I will have to let things remain this way.' You began to cry too. Then you sat on one of the steps and reached for your kerchief.

'I should go' you said after your tears have subsided. He nodded and looked away.

When you arrived at your home late in the afternoon, thick layers of clouds of dust has covered most of your furniture so you called your cleaner to book the next day but she was unusually cheerful that day. She had married and left Lagos but she could get you another cleaner in their company and the person was equally good. You congratulated her and declined the offer.

It only took few minutes to discover your kitchen apron which you wrapped around your body. You filled a bucket with water, wore a mask over your nose, slipped your palms into thin nylon gloves and set to clean your home.

With the aid of the mini ladder, you dusted the furniture and cobwebbed the walls. After you scrubbed the restroom until the dull ache in your bones invigorated your mind, you packed up the rest of Kachi's stuff into the box where such thing were put away. Sweat dripped under your breasts. It was therapeutic. Afterward, you pulled off your clothes and lay on the bed, exhausted. Later that night, you booked a next-day flight back to Abuja. The following week, you took up your new job as the head of chambers in your mother's firm.

The time came for Nnamdi to move to Jos. You went over and helped him pack up the things he would send to East and the ones he would be taking to his new residence.

'I still love you' he said while you rinsed your dusty palms in the kitchen sink after packing up the new and old utensils. You said nothing because you didn't know how to respond to such small talks anymore. But when the silence grew awkward, you found your voice.

'I took up a new job in town. I'm tired of staying idle.'

'Nice' he replied.

Another six months came and went by diligently. Your mother has finished building and furnishing her home in Otako and was ready to move, but you decided to go back to Lagos to move your properties and rent out the space, then move permanently to Abuja.

One morning in late October after your 35th birthday, while at work, you received Nnamdi's email.

Flawa,

I should have done this years ago before I moved back to England. I shouldn't have let you go the first time. I should have shown you how much I care about you. I should have loved you the way you deserved but we were so busy chasing dreams and careers that we ignored the most important things. You should visit Jos and see for yourself how pressing the demand for your portrait is. I had merely left it here after painting it and people do not mind buying the face of a stranger. I still have the one we painted earlier but it is for our eyes only; you and I. You don't have to overthink anything. Just acknowledge this message in any way you can and I will send you flight tickets for any day you wish. I have many great places to show you around here.

Nnamdi.

~~~~~~

ANOTHER SHORT RAP ON THE window jolts you back. Emilia peeked through the window.

'Flawa, what are you dreaming about? It is time' she said when you opened the door.
~~~~~~

'This car is not properly parked' you muttered on getting down.

'I will be back for it' she assured, straightening the hem of your dress.

'How are you feeling?' she asked, a naughty grin lurking in her eyes.

'You're beginning to act like my mother.' She laughed shortly, leading you away, towards the vestibule of the Marriage Registry.

I believe in putting thoughts together
I believe in writing them down
Let simple words convey them
Let unambiguity outline them
I am writing for a change,
a change in warped ideologies.
I am writing for peace
I hope you find peace in my words
I am writing for love
I want you to believe in the love you might
or never experience
I am writing for truth
I want you to be intentional
I am writing to reassure you
I hope you find purpose.

Chizitere Madeleine Nwaemesi

Acknowledgement

I am grateful to God for arming me with fortitude enough to last until the publication of this work.

To all the great authors whose books always inspired me to do better.

To my Editor, Akpa Arinzechukwu, thank you for your time.

To my father, Ebere Nwaemesi, my first and forever voluntary editor. Your library of powerful books, teachings, love, and support became a major source of mental elevation.

To my mother, Stella Nwaemesi, for always believing in my abilities.

To Vitus Nwaemesi, Chima Anyachebelu, Amara Anyachebelu, Estelle, and Pascal Chima, I love you all big time.

To Chidiebere Joseph, your counseling and undaunting support, morally and intellectually was never in vain.

To Chief Mrs. Doris Nwankwo, for all your support.

To Obiageli Iloakasia, you gave me the last push.

To my powerful league; Nkechi Obu, Chimoge Nwokolo, and Ijeoma Chinweze, for the love, moments of truth, laughter and memorable pictures. Let's keep working towards what we agreed on.

To Dimma Odezugo, idimma truly.

To Dr. Victor Nwasor, I appreciate you.

To Samuel Obidi, for making out time to read the initial draft of this work, willingly and giving out candid suggestions.

To Christopher Oduche, I did not forget your kind and thoughtful contribution to the progress of this work.

Finally, to everyone who has encouraged me in one way or the other towards the achievement of this piece, I appreciate you all.

CHIZITERE MADELEINE NWAEMESI is a writer, whose works have been published by Isele Magazine, Libretto Magazine, and elsewhere. She currently resides, and writes from Nigeria.